The Legend
ALASTAR

Bridget,
Thank you for
your
Ministry +
Friendship!

David
'21

DAVID N. CORRADO

MASCOT
BOOKS

www.mascotbooks.com

The Legend of Alastar

©2018 David N. Corrado. All Rights Reserved. No
part of this publication may be reproduced, stored
in a retrieval system or transmitted in any form by
any means electronic, mechanical, or photocopying,
recording or otherwise without the permission of
the author.

For more information, please contact:
Mascot Books
620 Herndon Parkway #320
Herndon, VA 20170
info@mascotbooks.com

Library of Congress Control Number: 2017960726

CPSIA Code: PRAF0118A
ISBN-13: 978-1-68401-751-5

Printed in China

The Legend of ALASTAR

story & art
DAVID N. CORRADO

special thank you
ALEXIS NEAPOLITAN JR.
JANE BUTKOVSKY
and Mom, for believing

Dedicated To:
Those afflicted by paralysis

I have always been inspired by actor Christopher Reeve, and his wife Dana, in their journey to find a cure.

May those suffering, and in need of hope, find strength and comfort, knowing tomorrow's cure for paralysis will come.

He turns toward the light...

...knowing the sound he has to follow.

ar from here and long ago,
an oft told tale you should know,
of knight errants and derring-do,
that once heard 'tis both bold and true.

Sinewy shadows in a crystal cave
for the young, or the pure of heart to save.
Emeralds providing eternal youth
to those who discover
magical truth.

Attend a warrior's
noble plight,
filled with adventure,
romance and might.
Set against the
emerald isle;
a fable of peril
and trial.

A man of virture
to admire
Someone to whom
all can aspire.
A brave and loving
warrior was he,
yet isolated from
all humanity.

Why would such
a noble man
cloak himself
where 'ere he can,
armoured to
provide a shell
respite from
his inner hell?

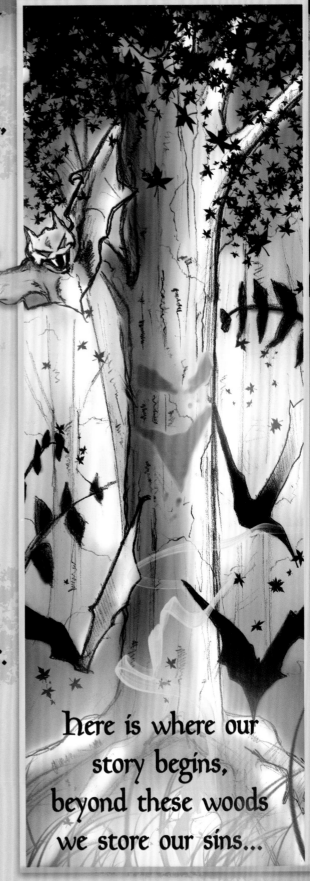

He masquerades
his dark
demon within,
shielding his pain
in order to win;
while hiding from
the ones he holds
so dear, eventually
creating a deep fear.

Alone is he in
hollow Wood,
striving to attain
common good.

Here is where our
story begins,
beyond these woods
we store our sins...

Once again little Dawn splashes her way just outside the kingdom.

To find a path she knows all too well.

To see a loved one whose hand always reaches out.

Like many evenings before, nine year old Dawn makes her way atop the highest hill overlooking the kingdom. here she always felt that the forest could actually speak to her, as she listened to the wind blow through the ancient trees.

The autumn hills are not all that overlooks Dawn's beautiful kingdom.

Standing at almost 20 feet, a guardian angel statue watches over the people; one arm bravely lifted for battle ... for protection.

While the other hand reaches out

Reaches out for guidance.

For hope.

For love.

As Dawn places the rose at the foot of the statue, she

To Dawn this statue means
more to her than it does to others.

She was told this statue was carved to represent her father's
passing, the night he gave his life for his country. For the past nine
years Dawn has wondered what her father was like.,

The autumn wind blows quickly through her golden hair as red leaves fall gently around her. It isn't too long before she realizes this time she is not alone on her journey.

She has someone special watching over her.

Her grandfather loves her. He makes sure she is happy and has everything she wants.

Almost everything.

Once more her grandfather, Godfrey, explains he cannot always keep up with her when she runs up those hills. He then tells her to stop scaring off all the foxes. She laughs. Then as quick as a bird, she grabs a shiny dagger tucked inside her grandfather's belt.

It's the one thing he can't give her, and she knows that. Stopping suddenly, Dawn looks up at her grandfather and asks...

this was my father's dagger wasn't it?

Little girls don't often want such things, but Dawn is different!

She slowly gives it back.

I KNOW HE WOULD WANT YOU TO HAVE HIS SPECIAL DAGGER, BUT NOT JUST YET!

He then explains...

YOUR FATHER WAS A VERY NOBLE MAN. MANY LOVED HIM.

HE WAS BRAVE WHEN OTHERS WERE NOT.

grumpa, would he remember me?

At first Godfrey only smiles.
Then looking up at the statue he tells Dawn...

YOUR FATHER ALWAYS KNEW YOU WERE SPECIAL. HE COULDN'T WAIT FOR YOU TO BE BORN!

AND I GAVE HIM THIS DAGGER THE DAY HE WAS KNIGHTED!

"HE DOES REMEMBER YOU DAWN. HE IS UP ABOVE, WATCHING THE BEAUTIFUL WOMAN YOU ARE BECOMING."

i love your stories grumpa.

just like the ones uncle jerald tells me.

The once lit heavenly statue goes dim as the final ray of sunlight sets. Night has fallen early for Dawn and Godfrey. Most nights they are able to find their way home in the dark.

This is not one of them.

A certain evil has found its way.

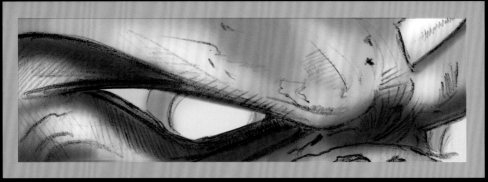

For Dawn and her grandfather have been out much too late.

HA! "MY SON JERALD DOES LOVE TO TELL STORIES!"

"BUT MINE HAPPEN TO BE TRUE YOUNG LADY!"

SNAP

All at once fear has taken over. Dawn no longer feels safe.

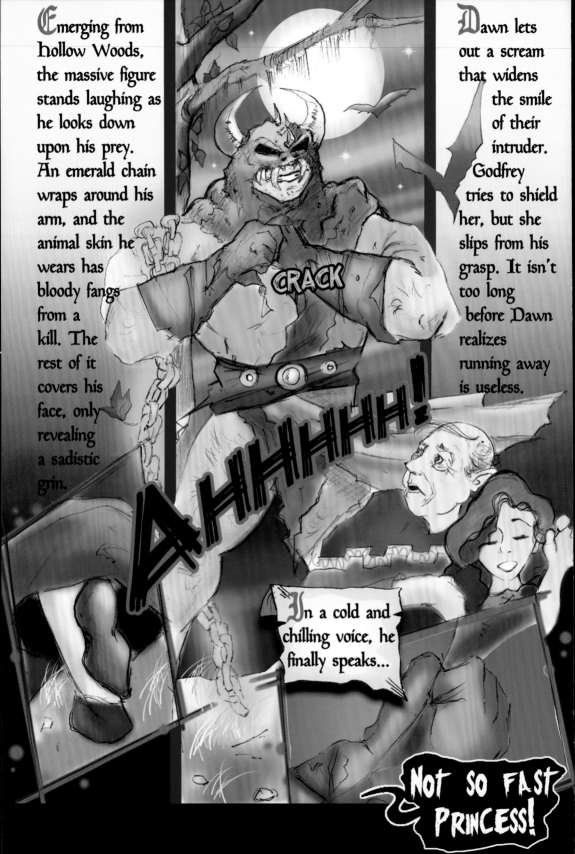

Emerging from hollow Woods, the massive figure stands laughing as he looks down upon his prey. An emerald chain wraps around his arm, and the animal skin he wears has bloody fangs from a kill. The rest of it covers his face, only revealing a sadistic grin.

Dawn lets out a scream that widens the smile of their intruder. Godfrey tries to shield her, but she slips from his grasp. It isn't too long before Dawn realizes running away is useless.

CRACK

AHHHHHH!

In a cold and chilling voice, he finally speaks...

NOT SO FAST PRINCESS!

By the time Godfrey turns around, the attacker is gone.

Yet the voice still remains.

"SHE WILL SERVE HER PURPOSE WELL!"

He looks up at the statue, and remembers all it stands for.

Bats stare and grin, laughing at the tragedy recently befallen unto him.

Beside the crushed rose petals, he cries.

"ISABEL... WHAT HAVE I DONE??"

"WHAT HAVE I DONE?"

Dawn's mother Isabel, unaware of her daughter's predicament, awaits her arrival.

The moonlight shines down upon her undeniable beauty.

Many who know Isabel know her talents include the making of stained glass. Her latest, a depicition of an armoured knight, will soon grace the king's castle. Tonight she sleeps in the cottage where Dawn's father lived. It has now become her studio for creating art. While working there she can't help thinking of Dawn's father, who she always regarded as her one true soulmate.

She thinks of their journey inside a crystal cave. She remembers how compeled they were to follow a sound that led them to a waterfall within the forest. Upon finding the cave, they came upon two unique gems that when held next to each other, displayed every possible color.

Deciding to keep the treasures, Isabel said they should be worn around their necks, symbolizing their friendship.

As time went on they fell in love.

Not too long after, Dawn was born.

Nevertheless something terrible took Isabel's love and left Dawn fatherless...

Yearning for her lost love, Isabel was comforted by Prince Gabriel. he took her and Dawn in, and has looked after them as his own family ever since.

She loves Gabriel, but has not told him how she found the crystal.
She worries there are things he wouldn't understand.
Staring deep into her knight's eyes, she wonders...
...what would the man behind the armour really look like?
Her questions would have to wait.
ISABEL! I COULDN'T SAVE HER!
SHE'S GONE!
FATHER!
YOU'RE BLEEDING!

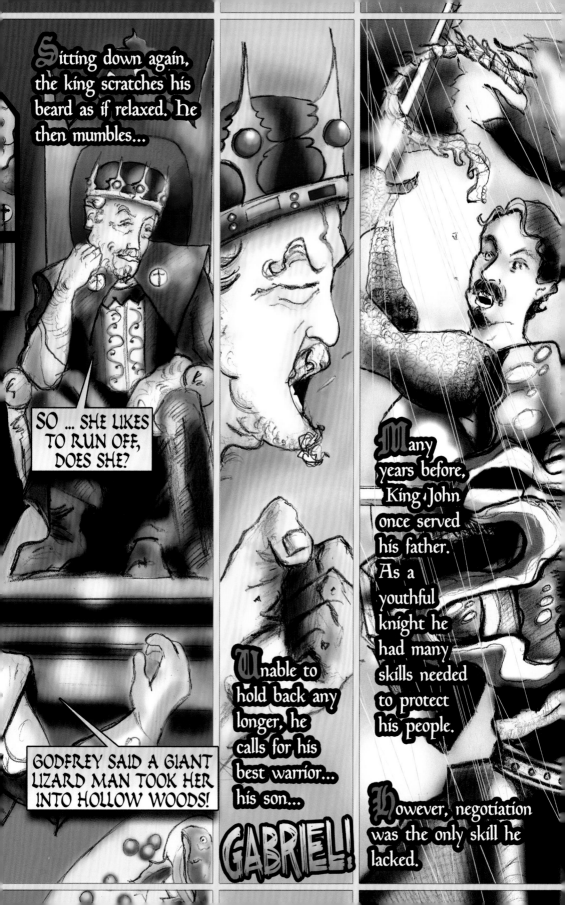

Sitting down again, the king scratches his beard as if relaxed. He then mumbles...

SO ... SHE LIKES TO RUN OFF, DOES SHE?

GODFREY SAID A GIANT LIZARD MAN TOOK HER INTO HOLLOW WOODS!

Unable to hold back any longer, he calls for his best warrior... his son...

GABRIEL!

Many years before, King John once served his father. As a youthful knight he had many skills needed to protect his people.

However, negotiation was the only skill he lacked.

The king has always used his knowledge of warfare to protect the land. His family's castle rests high atop an ancient mountain, which rises above the village. Tonight his men will embark on a journey to bring back a young girl who holds a special place in the kingdom's heart. A bridge ascends, leading the knights into the moonlit valley...

Leading the royal army, as he has many times before, is Prince Gabriel.

Only one word echoes in him.

Dawn.

Gabriel's young squire, Philip, rides at his side. To his right is Isabel's older brother Jerald, who is always ready to aid the prince.

Tonight is one night they never foresaw.

MOVE FORWARD!
WE SEARCH EVERY
CORNER OF THIS
KINGDOM!

High above his tower, King John and Queen Katherine hold hands as they watch the army search every corner of the village below. Not many can say they saw a tear fall from the king's eyes. As the cold night carries on, the hours seem like days. Isabel feels the fear race down her back, alone and in terror.

Morning comes, and the army must answer to the king. In his private chapel, King John sits before them. his eyes are glazed, with his left hand draped over his knee as though it had not moved in hours. As they approach him, they hear his chilling voice echo throughout the halls of the room.

He speaks briefly, but is to the point...

"WHERE'S THE GIRL?"

On this day, Isabel will always be haunted by her husband's eyes. How they looked as he promised her.

She will remember how he held her hand.

The same way Dawn's father once did.

I BEG YOU MY LOVE, WAIT HERE UNTIL MY ARRIVAL. DAWN WILL BE WITH ME. SHE IS MY DAUGHTER NOW TOO, MY LIFE!

The wind feels colder than the day before, as even more leaves blanket the pathways. Gabriel reaches down, giving Isabel a final kiss. his horse then pulls back.

PLEASE STAY WITH YOUR FATHER, YOU BOTH ARE WELL GUARDED.

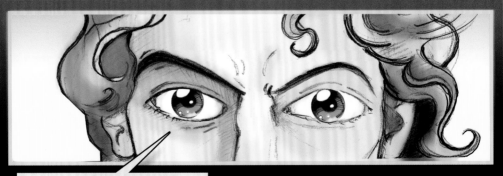

THE ABANDONED TAVERN IS FORBIDDEN!

As his eyes begin to form tears, Jerald can't help but feel his sister's pain.

Moments later they ride quickly to a part of the kingdom most would rather avoid.

They search for an elder woman who Gabriel has banned from the public.

For black magic

and treason.

Suddenly their horse stops after picking up an unusual scent.

Even in daylight the once popular town tavern has an eerie look to it as it sits in isolation. It appears to be ready to crumble at any moment. Cracks run down the stone structure like scars that will never heal.

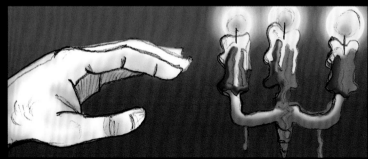

An emerald door appears slightly open. Jerald leads his sister inside with the hopes that the one they search for will be there. Just a few feet in, a candle appears recently lit.

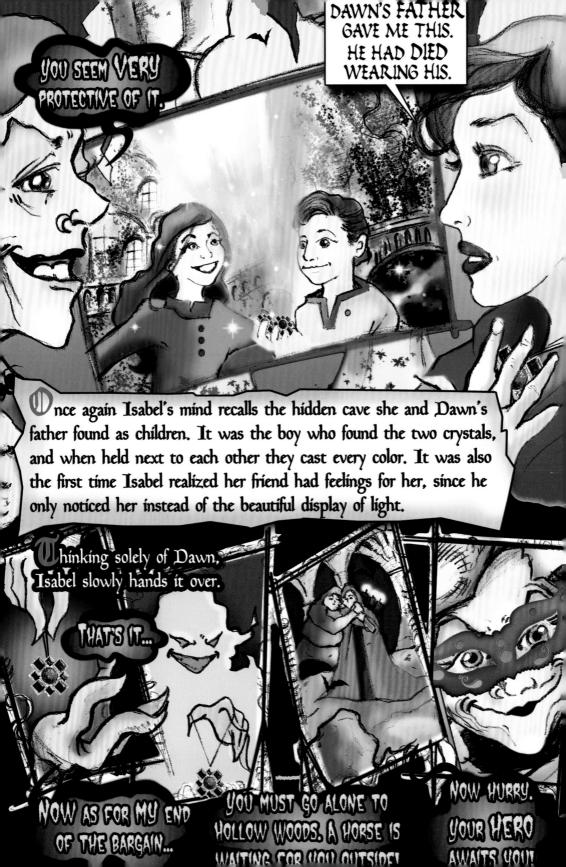

Following Silvia's orders, Isabel says farewell to her brother as they stand before hollow Woods. It has been years since she has ventured into the depths of this forest. The wind suddenly whistles as it blows the tree branches in the direction she is to go.

Minutes pass as seemingly an eternity to her.

Nervous and afraid, Isabel still rides on, never losing sight of her mission.

By now the sun has reached its peak. As noon arrives, she has traveled almost an hour.

The clattering hooves of Silvia's horse are almost in perfect rhythm with Isabel's heartbeat. With every step she imagines Dawn alone with that monster, while praying she is still alive.

Wishing Silvia had told her more, Isabel looks for any sign of a man in crystal armour. She wants to believe in her aunt, but an uncertain feeling envelopes her about this hidden warrior many know so little about. her worried mind then hears the sound of wings flapping in the distance.

Suddenly those flapping wings form a demonic shape, leaving Isabel truly alone.

The hot afternoon sun beats down upon Isabel's back as the cool autumn wind runs through her hair. Despite her valiant effort, she lies on the ground, her heart still beating but no longer aware of her surroundings.

The poison from the bite has traveled into her bloodstream and rendered her unconscious. It would seem to any onlooker that her quest to find her daughter has finally come to an end; and with each passing moment, her life may also end.

From where they are, the mysterious warrior can
hear Gabriel and his men enter the woods. He looks down upon
Isabel, not knowing why this woman entered such a dangerous
place on her own. He knows she does not have much time left,
after noticing blood trickle down her neck from the venomous bite.
He then carefully picks her up, his crystal armour shining while
his horse in similiar armour leads the way.

After she gloats, Silvia puts on Isabel's necklace. Her skin then becomes pale and soft, and her dress like new.

Her mind is then flooded with memories from her dark past, but not every memory is dark...

Silvia once was a happy child, but no one could control her interest in black magic. Her deadly desires began to take over. As a young girl, she mastered the dark arts. Her beauty even helped her seduce a loving warlock.

They were happily wed and had a son. The warlock showed Silvia the rewards of using their sorceries for good. However, as the years went by her love became deathly ill, and knew he couldn't save himself.

He then turned into a dragon to fly off and die. Silvia soon became obsessed with aging and death. She began to search for the cave that contained the magical crystals she dreamt of as a child.

In time, the anger she hid for so long surfaced again. This had caused her to lose hope in seeing her true love again in the afterlife.

As she grew older, she realized only the pure of heart can find the cave. She used the magic she had to keep her aging body alive. Fifteen years ago she learned of two children who found crystals there.

In befriending young Isabel, Silvia lied in telling her she was her aunt. Soon more sorcery led to Gabriel exiling her. Keeping a close eye on Isabel, she and her son waited for the right time to attack Dawn. Unlike Isabel, Silvia knew the necklace and right combination of magic can make one younger. She also knew the cave would supply the rest for her evil desires.

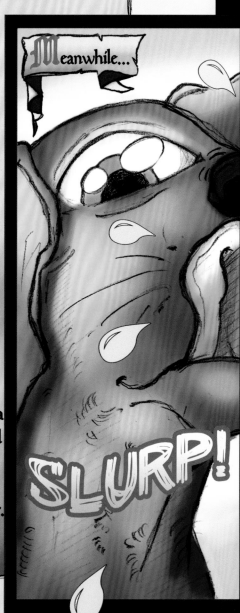

Meanwhile...

SLURP!!

breeze spins Isabel around, facing her toward a cliff overlooking this strange world. She notices crumbled structures that once stood, and are now falling into decay of what could have been an ancient civilization lost long ago. The faint lights in the distance give hints that this world

Long ago some might have called this home. Now left alone and forgotten, only one seems to live here. Isabel's eyes are drawn back to the long flowing cloak of her rescuer. While still remaining silent, he stands before her with his arms crossed as if waiting for an explanation. Staying within the shadows, his armour still glows

Much to Isabel's surprise it appears her hero seems lost and distant.

Yet high above them, Gabriel and his men are thrown from their horses as vines quickly slither from the earth below. Wrapping tightly around each of them, they struggle to get free of its poisonious barbs.

Isabel once again tries to reach out to the armoured figure. She doesn't realize just how much energy he used in order to heal her body from the venomous bite. She is also unaware that his power is charged by the large crystal she saw in the far

MIGHT BE DEAD AND YOU JUST WALK AWAY?

WHO ARE YOU REALLY?

his squire, but finds it's too late as the vines pull them closer. These vines move in a slow, but powerful manner that not even the army's horses can escape.

Alastar finally responds to Isabel, but not in the way she had imagined. his voice is calm, but slightly gives away his years of despair and isolation. One might ask why would such a noble man cloak himself where'ere he can? What would it take for Isabel to find the hero within him so many of her kingdom's people have told tales about? What is it that holds him back from being

$\mathcal{G}$abriel, Philip, and the rest of the army finally give into the force of the vines that have them pinned against an aged tree. Their horses join them, feeling nothing but hopelessness as the heavy burden of this strange growth weighs down upon them.

$\mathcal{I}$n one final attempt, Isabel whispers what is truly on her mind regarding her only child. To her dismay, Alastar still appears distant as he sits upon his armoured horse looking off into the far distance. After she speaks her final words, Isabel grabs the sides of her rose colored cloak and begins to head off, not sure as to where to go from here. Miles below hollow Woods, Isabel has found herself in a world she never knew existed, and without the help of her rescuer she may never reach her world in time.

THAT MONSTER COULD BE HURTING DAWN RIGHT NOW!

Human-like trees whistle, a chilling wind blows, and a young woman tries to escape it all. Hopeless, she runs from who she thought was a hero. Completely lost and alone, Isabel tries to contain her fear once again.

BARK
BARK

She looks up and sees the sky from her home, feeling as if she's in a world within a world.

UGH!

OHHH MY PUPPET, YOU WILL COME TO KNOW THEE WELL!
I HAVE BEEN WATCHING YOU A VERY LONG TIME.
I HAVE COME TO KNOW YOU BETTER THAN YOU KNOW THYSELF!
SUCH A SHAME YOU HAD TO USE PRECIOUS POWER TO CURE YOUR NEW FRIEND!

On command Ava takes a giant leap forward. Isabel will soon come to realize nothing has prepared her for these next few moments.

Hurdling miiles above the ground, Isabel somehow trusts this stranger.

They ride past fallen rocks while making their way to the next island in the sunlit sky.

Isabel's eyes widen as they land on a path that takes them straight into the unknown.

Alas nothing can be seen in the distance, only a white mist leaving behind the crystal glints of a strange and forgotten world.

Finally arriving back in hollow Woods, all looks the same as they left it.

LET'S WELCOME OUR FRIEND BACK BY TESTING HIS UNBREAKABLE ARMOUR, SHALL WE?

RELEASE MY SLIMES!

RRRPT!

BARRH!

The eerie roads of hollow Woods take them to the edge of the
forest where Dawn was last seen. The country hills then turn
into walkways that lead to the kingdom's main street. Puddles
filled with reflections of the afternoon sky are interrupted by the
hooves of Ava's feet. They swiftly ride past the excited villagers

By now everyone knows of Dawn's disappearance. The people gathering quickly begin to chant for Alastar, feeling relief that the kingdom once again has his aid. Since Gabriel has chosen Isabel as his future queen, she has been used to the cheering of crowds, however, nothing has prepared her for this kind of reaction.

The sounds of breaking bones and shattered ribs echo throughout the aged tavern. The old man in the corner can't help but occasionally peek at the brutality inflicted by one man.

Past the twisted torsos, Isabel finds her way back to that spiral staircase she knew as a child. She believed Silvia to be her aunt, who told fantasic tales of magic, brave warriors, and ancient crystals. Now all of that has come to an end, once she realizes it was all a lie.

Her child's leather boot.

Proof that Dawn was there.

GOD HAVE MERCY!

All that can be heard throughout the empty cave is the fluttering of bat wings and water dripping from above.

Fear consumes Isabel as she realizes Dawn's boot was covered in slime blood.

Crystals once again light up the pillars as though their arrival was predicted.

The pillars begin showing that Dawn is still alive. Somewhere...

DAWN!

Hidden behind the glowing pillar, Slvia watches her prey.

She then uses her magic to transform into a hybrid snake...

...Slithering up Alastar's armour as though she already knew its design.

AAAARGH!

HA HA HA HA HA HA HA HA HA HA HA HA HA

...she then slithers off.

YOU ... YOU'RE HURT?!

After a loud laugh...

As the venom bite weakens his body, Alastar, for the first time in years, feels pain.

As Isabel helps Alastar to his feet, she looks up toward the long twisted stairs they now have to climb.

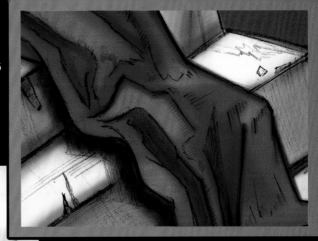

Each step harder than the last, Isabel wonders why his cape has to be as long as it is.

SWOOOSH!

Riding off, she leads Ava to a place Silvia had forgotten about. A place Isabel calls home.

A place beyond the castle and busy village streets.

A place outside the kingdom's reach.

The past nine years she has lived in the castle with Gabriel...

...yet before that, this cottage was her home.

A home where she and Dawn's father could grow old together.

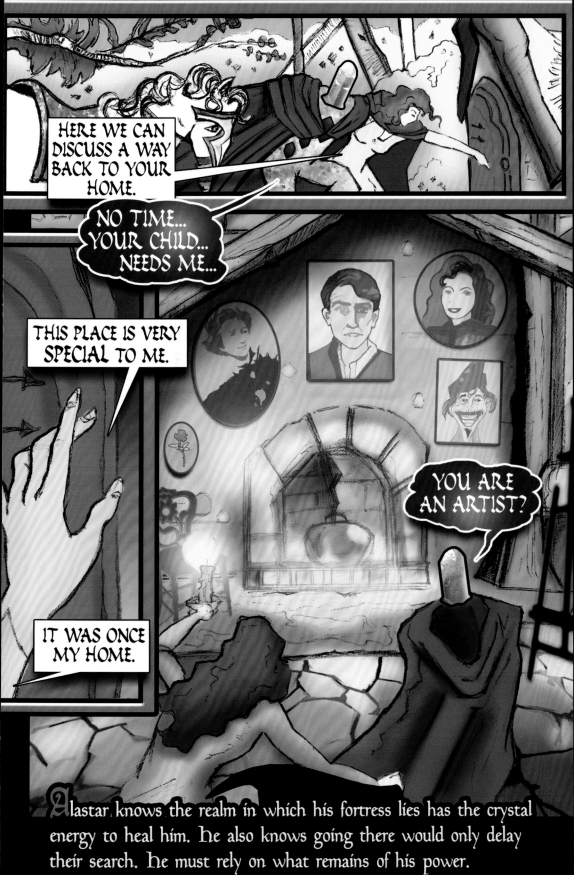

Alastar knows the realm in which his fortress lies has the crystal energy to heal him. he also knows going there would only delay their search. he must rely on what remains of his power.

The night drifts on as loneliness and
fear consume Isabel's thoughts.

She
wonders
who the
armoured
man is
down the
hall.

The cold
wind
blows as
more
questions
haunt her
mind.

Can he
really
save
Dawn?

Knowing this is the second night
wondering the fate of her only child.

Of all the kingdom's children, **WHY** Dawn?

Is it because of their aquired royalty?

How long has Silvia been planning this evil plot?

Why would she summon this enigmatic warrior?

AND...

What does he look like behind the armour?

CREEEK

As Isabel's eyes are fixed on her friend, her arm taps the wooden door creating a sound that breaks the silence. Before Alastar can turn around, she is already half way down the hall to her bedroom. her questions would have to wait.

A chilling scream followed by the sound of a broken spine is heard during the early morning hours throughout the village. The singer's wagon now belongs to a new owner who begins to load it up with a heavy locked chest. Only he can hear the wimpering sounds of a child that come from within. The wheels take off as an even younger Silvia smiles in delight.

They finally arrive by evening. The mist slowly reveals the century-old cathedral in the near distance, standing almost eerie and alone.

They left behind a kingdom that will soon behold the power Silvia obtained from the necklace.

Waiting for Alastar to be far enough away, she sets loose her army of slimes,

while Gabriel, backed by his army, believe he has the witch cornered.

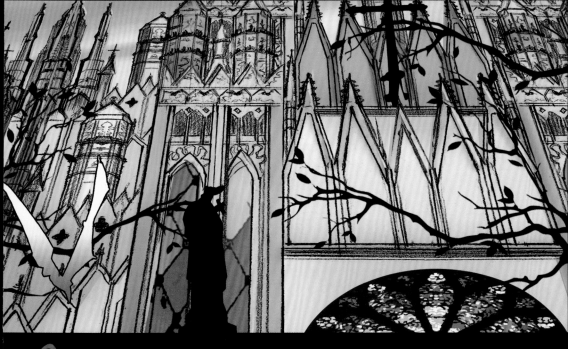

Not much time has passed before silence has taken over. Alastar keeps Isabel behind him as he looks over the cathedral. He tries to find another entrance inside which avoids the main door. He knows Dawn is inside and needs his help. He also senses something powerful awaits him there. Meanwhile, Isabel waits as told. She can't help but once again wonder what lies beneath the warrior's mysterious armour.

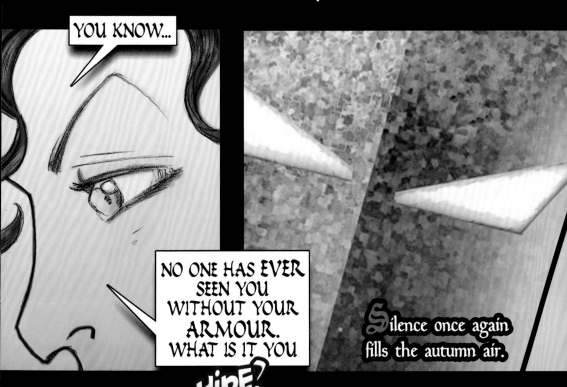

YOU KNOW...

NO ONE HAS EVER SEEN YOU WITHOUT YOUR ARMOUR. WHAT IS IT YOU HIDE?

Silence once again fills the autumn air.

WE'LL ARRIVE AT THAT CATHDERAL BY MORNING!

WHOEVER SILVIA'S SON IS, THAT'S WHO WE'RE UP AGAINST!

OUR ONLY PRIORITY IS RESUCING DAWN AND ISABEL! I KNOW NOT OF ALASTAR'S INTENTIONS!

AAAHH!

From where they are, a deadly and urgent cry for help is heard coming from the village, followed by several more. The sound of children screaming and smoke rising make Gabriel realize it might be even longer before he reaches his step-daughter.

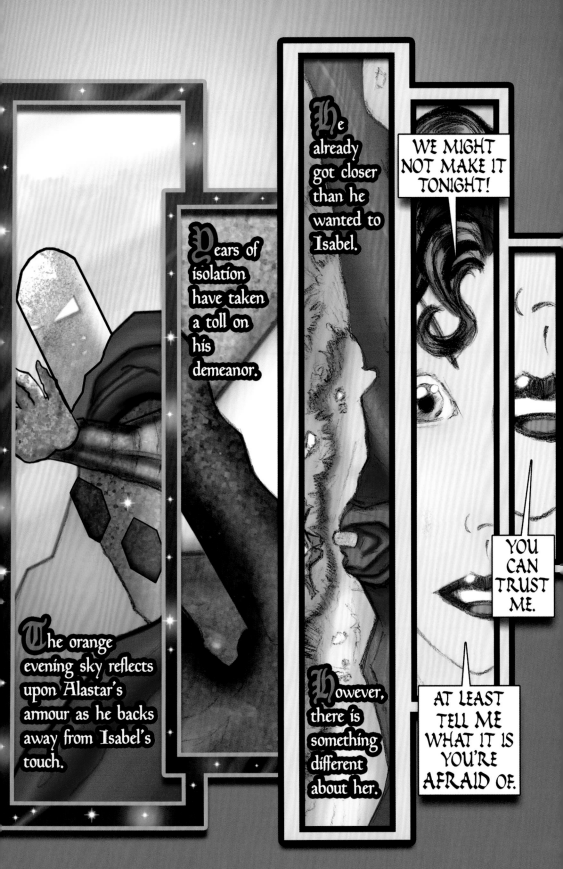

The orange evening sky reflects upon Alastar's armour as he backs away from Isabel's touch.

Years of isolation have taken a toll on his demeanor.

He already got closer than he wanted to Isabel.

However, there is something different about her.

WE MIGHT NOT MAKE IT TONIGHT!

YOU CAN TRUST ME.

AT LEAST TELL ME WHAT IT IS YOU'RE AFRAID OF.

Longingly staring into the conflicted warrior's hollowed eyes, Isabel wonders when the silence will end.

Oddly, Alastar wonders if she can even care for him.

Violent autumn winds pick up as Alastar once again pulls back, looking to the shadows.

Eventually he gives in.

NONE OF US EVER KNEW.

I WON'T TELL A SOUL.

ONLY ON THE INSIDE.

DOES IT HURT?

His eyes struggle to look at Isabel's. As he looks away she reaches for his hand. She notices his face seems as though he lived hundreds of years searching for something lost, only to never have found it. All the years of isolation he was never seen without his armour. The only thing that separates him from the rest of Silvia's slimes is his free will. The crystal armour shields his mind from her control, which has always fueled her rage.

The moment ends as a cry for help is heard coming from the cathedral.

NOOOOO!

DAWN?

Soon enough a warrior gathers his thoughts, puts on his armour, and makes his way to the main doors. The only sound to be heard upon opening the door is a long unwelcomed creek echoing throughout an empty century-old cathedral.

The eerie scream gets louder and louder as the pair make their way to the top of the stairs. They have climbed stairs like these just a day earlier, and now they will climb together once more. For the first time, Alastar truly feels his armour weighing down upon him.

He knows not what he will find behind the top door, but senses it will come at a cost. his body is weary. he feels the venom still flowing through his veins, ready to inflict pain at any moment. however, he continues as if he was meant to help Isabel, like an angel sent to guide her during the darkest of her days.

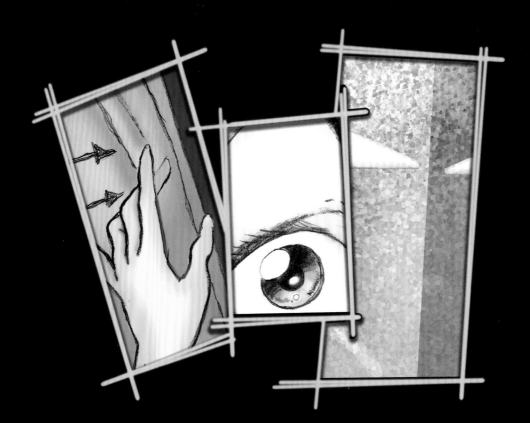

At the top, a door is opened.

Despite no windows, a sudden chill is felt.

A small child then turns her head and softy whispers...

momma?

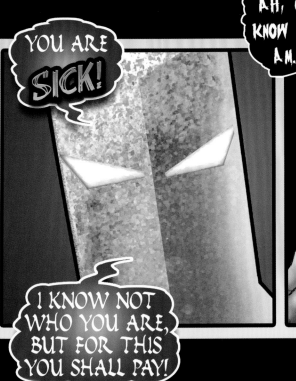

Isabel accepts a nod from Alastar and guides Dawn downstairs. She is finally free to go. She has found her daughter, and can now continue with her life. However, she does not want to leave Alastar in his weakened state, fearing it may be the last she sees of him.

As she leaves, she hears Alastar walk over to Dawn's abductor. He delivers the first blow, while Shade responds with nothing more than a grim smile.

KRAK

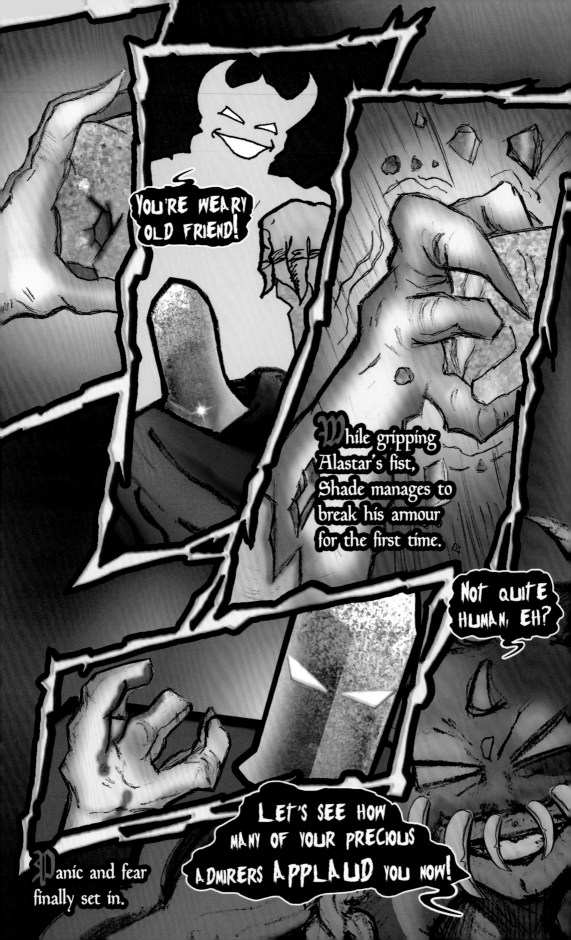

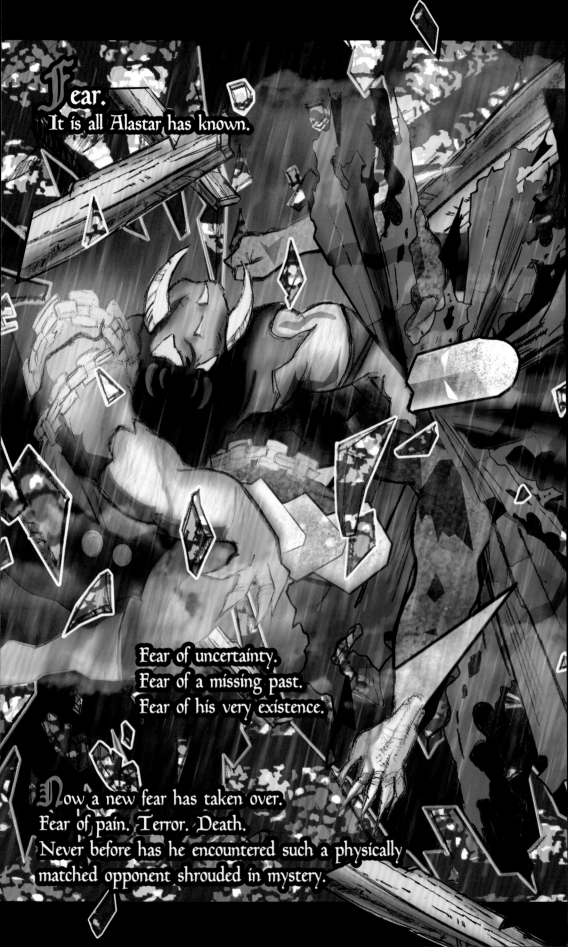

Fear.
It is all Alastar has known.

Fear of uncertainty.
Fear of a missing past.
Fear of his very existence.

Now a new fear has taken over.
Fear of pain. Terror. Death.
Never before has he encountered such a physically matched opponent shrouded in mystery.

...AND MURDERED EVERY LAST ONE OF THOSE INHABITANTS...

...LONG BEFORE YOU PUT ON THEIR ARMOUR.

Shade briefly reverts to a lizard-like form to inflict more terror unto his victim.

"THE DWARFS WHO GUARDED THOSE CRYSTALS WITH WATCHFUL EYES..."

...WILL NEVER AGAIN SEE THE LIGHT OF DAY!

When smoke from the blast clears, Shade turns to find his enemy shrouded among the statues atop the cathedral. Alastar's energy has been drained, rendering him to combat.

The two seem like angered giants as Isabel and Dawn watch from below. As the rain falls heavier, they struggle to see their hero hang on for his life. All at once a loud bolt strikes as Alastar takes another blow. This time a small crystal detaches from his armour. It is quickly lit by the lighting as it flies upward.

Dawn is held back by her mother as she tries to reach her father. She is not yet aware of their connection, but Isabel finally realizes her true love has fallen once again. It seems a life in solitude wasn't enough. Now strong emerald chains pierce his beast-like flesh that was once protected from crystal armour. his head spins. his eyes barely regain their focus.

Due to his pure heart, the crystal saved Alastar after he was attacked by his jealous friend nine years ago on this very night. Although it could not break Silvia's curse, the crystal around his neck provided mystical armour that would hide his beast appearance. Finally he recalls everything...

MY BROKEN LIMBS MIGHT BE OF USE...

...THEY'LL HELP ME FORGET THE PAIN.

THE PAIN OF THIS WITCH'S CURSE...

...A CURSE THAT STOLE MY NAME.

I HAVE FINALLY BEEN AWAKENED...

...WITH NOWHERE LEFT TO GO.

I CAN SEE YOU FROM AFAR...

...YOU SEEM AS THOUGH YOU KNOW.

YET THERE IS SO MUCH PAIN...
...PAIN I NEVER KNEW BEFORE.
IT WAS ME THEY WERE AFTER...
...AND MY SPIRIT THEY TORE.
BUT I WONT LET GO...
...I WONT LET YOU GO...
...I'M NOT LETTING YOU GO.

YET THERE IS SO MUCH PAIN...

...PAIN I NEVER KNEW BEFORE...

IT WAS ME THEY WERE AFTER...

...AND MY SPIRIT THEY TORE.

A few hours later the sun rises.
Gabriel and his cavalry arrive to find themselves too late...

A chilling wind blows through the tree branches as morning finds its way. Despite the night's bitterness, a rainbow breaks through the clouds ending in the far distance. Now with Silvia captured, the souls she tortured will ultimately find peace. As for Alastar, he too found an end to his curse. At the cost of his life, he finally remembered his family and the life he once had.

A festival soon welcomes all to the castle to celebrate.

As Dawn recovers, she joins the week long gathering in her honor. Like her father, she too will hide the curse inflicted upon her by covering half her face.

Gabriel vows to spend the rest of his life searching for a cure. No matter what it takes.

Gabriel's efforts in saving the kingdom will never be forgotten. Without his leadership, their world would have fallen to despair. The king's doubts about Alastar also vanish, as he finally regards him as a hero.

They believe Isabel when she says that Alastar is Dawn's father. A man who was cursed into isolation shortly after her birth.

She also finishes her depiction of the knight.

This one unshattered.

That night she looked up to the brightly lit sky...

...while others are celebrating, she remembers her love.

Meanwhile, beneath the castle's surface lies an especially dark place. Silvia will now call it her home until the king decides her fate.

Spring.

Once more life has returned to the valley.

Even on days as beautiful as today, Dawn still struggles to live with her monstrous curse.

Isabel's crystal lies within Silvia's cave, so she wears a different one;

Undoubtedly her trips to the statue overlooking the kingdom mean so much more now. She finally knows the fate of her father.

the same one that powered unbreakable armour. She relives her first kiss, her true love. Dawn's father. Alastar.

All at once a sudden warm breeze is felt. Dawn's new dog senses a presence in the far distance and lets out a loud bark. Everyone turns quickly...

Once the spring pollen clears and a faint mist rises, the royal family is greeted by a familiar friend in the distance. A restored Alastar, still keeping his distance, stands many feet from Dawn and her family. They can't believe their eyes as Ava lets out a loud neigh, showing everyone she too is alive and well. They quickly notice a spirtual glow surrounding Alastar and his horse, as though their spirits were sent from above.

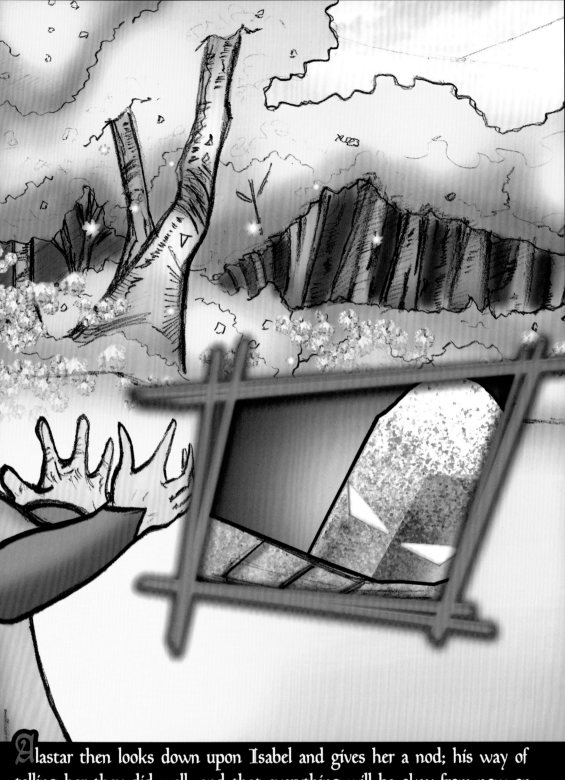

Alastar then looks down upon Isabel and gives her a nod; his way of telling her they did well, and that everything will be okay from now on. Isbael doesn't understand what is happening, but still gives Dawn's father a slight smile. What comes next is sure to be remembered by young Dawn for the rest of her life. As the royal family continues to stare in amazement, Alastar reaches for the base of his helmet...

When Daniel hears heavenly spirits call his name, he turns toward the light...

...knowing the sound he has to follow.

He leaves with a smile, realizing Isabel and Dawn will be cared for by Gabriel.

Reflecting on his life, it was not the one he wanted. All he wished for was a quiet life with Isabel.

Despite the curse brought unto him, he still became a hero, a guardian to those who needed one.

For now he can't be with his true love. However, he does not know what the future, or the afterlife will bring. He rides away, finally free of all the demons who pulled him down the past nine years, leaving behind unbreakable armour that once shielded his fear.

In a final sprint, Ava lifts off. The two suddenly fade into the evening sky, leaving behind the world they loved so much.

The portal to the cave Daniel and Isabel found as children closes, until another child pure of heart stumbles upon it.

thank you.

Daniel will be with his loved ones, who passed on before him.

He will finally meet members from that lost civilization that once occupied the hidden realm he called his home.

For it was their armour that made him Alastar, protector of men.

Years from now, the royal family will look back and remember. Reminiscing about a very special time.

However, Dawn will come to realize the danger in reminiscing...

...lies behind nostalgic eyes.

There can be no tomorrow...

Till yesterday is left behind.

Nostalgia comes to haunt us, every few years, or so;
Seeking fond memories of a yesterday that has gone.

Although the present exists in the shadow of the past...

The future cannot erase a present whose only claim is its past.

The END

The Legend of ALASTAR

DAVID N. CORRADO

Cast of Characters

All main characters in *The Legend of Alastar* are inspired by real people.

ALASTAR/DANIEL- Daniel Corrado

ISABEL- In Memory of Marie Corrado

DAWN- Margaret Mihalick

SHADE- Cody Schade

GABRIEL- Christopher Krupilis

JERALD- Robert Houseknecht

SQUIRE- Philip Corrado

GODFREY- Leo Lopo

KING- John P. Charles

QUEEN- Katherine Corrado

In Character

Christopher Krupilis

Margaret Mihalick

Robert Houseknecht

Leo Lopo

My mother, Katherine Corrado

Cody Schade

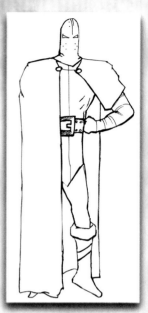

First Sketch '09

Daniel Corrado

A photo shoot was held a few years before publication. The models dressed in character and acted out scenes I would later illustrate. Above, Chris Krupilis, the model for Gabriel, also wore Alastar's costume while Margaret Mihalick posed next to him as young Dawn. My brother Daniel was unknowingly the inspiration for the title hero, Alastar.

About the Author

David N. Corrado is a fine artist and illustrator from northeast Pennsylvania. At a young age, his maternal grandfather introduced him to the art of drawing and painting.

After graduating from Penn State University, he went on to complete altar paintings for churches, portraits for R/C Theaters, and murals for both an American Legion and a town hall.

"The Legend of Alastar" is his first work of fiction. As the writer and illustrator, he hopes his book will be enjoyed by future generations.

His past and current work can be viewed online under "Artist Gallery of David N. Corrado" and "The Legend of Alastar," both on Facebook. He may be contacted at davidc993@yahoo.com.